"Life is like riding a bicycle. To keep your balance you must keep moving."

"The only reason for time is so that everything doesn't happen at once."

"Joy in looking and comprehending is nature's most beautiful gift."

"Anyone who has never made a mistake has never tried anything new."

# Ask Albert Einstein

## Lynne Barasch

FRANCES FOSTER BOOKS • FARRAR, STRAUS AND GIROUX • NEW YORK

In 1952, I was seven years old, and my big sister,
Annabel, was fifteen. Eisenhower was running for president,

and Albert Einstein was the most famous scientist
and mathematician in the world. He still is.

Annabel was always
my best friend. She
taught me everything:

how to ride my bike,

how to roller-skate,

even how to make Toll House cookies. And she pretended
not to notice when I ate some of the chocolate chips.

As good as Annabel was at everything, there was one thing that stumped her: math. She tried hard, even went to extra-help math class every day before school began, but still got a D in math on her report card.

One day, Annabel came home from school with tears in her eyes. "The teacher says I have one last chance to get a passing grade in math." She waved a paper at me crying, "I have to solve this problem in two weeks or else! Who does she think I am, Albert Einstein?" I didn't know who that was, but the very next day I found out.

One of the kids in my school brought in a photo for show-and-tell. "This is Albert Einstein, the most famous scientist and mathematician in the world.

Oo Pp Qq Rr Ss Tt Uu Vv Ww Xx Yy Zz

He figured out the theory of relativity in a room all by himself, doing math on his blackboard." I looked at the photo. Albert Einstein was old. He had kind eyes.

When I got home, I ran up to our room. I could hear Annabel, but the door was closed. I knew she was working on her math problem. Every few minutes I heard her say things like "Oh no! External tangent? This can't be right!" and "I don't get it! I just don't get it!"

Finally, she came out looking crushed. I tried to comfort her. "Now I know who Albert Einstein is," I told her. "He used to do all his math on his blackboard alone in his room." Annabel growled. "And he's still at it, for all the good that does me!" Still at it? I thought. I had to know more about Albert Einstein. What is his theory of relativity? Since Annabel is my relative, maybe he could help her.

I went to the library. The librarian showed me where to find books about Albert Einstein. He was born in Germany in 1879. In the early 1930s, he realized that Adolf Hitler was a threat to Jews living in Germany, especially to himself, a world-famous Jewish scientist.

So in 1932, he came to America and never returned to Germany.

There was a picture of Albert Einstein in front of his house in Princeton, New Jersey. He worked and taught there at the Institute for Advanced Study.

Then there was a lot of confusing stuff. I didn't understand it but I wrote it down. Albert Einstein demonstrated that measurements of time and distance vary systematically as anything moves relative to anything else. We live in space-time, not space and time. Matter bends space-time. In 1919, this theory was tested by British astronomers who observed a total solar eclipse and proved Einstein was right.

There was even a letter Albert wrote to his mother saying, "The English expedition has really proved that light is deviated by the Sun." What did this mean? If Albert Einstein figured all that out, he could surely solve Annabel's math problem. But would he?

Later, at home, I made a careful copy of the math problem in my
notebook when Annabel wasn't looking. Then I wrote this letter:

Dear Albert Einstein,

My sister Annabel is 15. She has a lot of trouble with math. But she can do everything else in the world. Annabel will fail math if she doesn't get this problem right, and she tries so hard. I bet you can do it. Will you? Please send the answer soon.

Her sister, April

P.S. I'm in 2nd grade.
Here is Annabel's problem:
The common external tangent of two tangent circles of radii 8 inches and 2 inches is?

I put the letter in an envelope and wrote ALBERT EINSTEIN, PRINCETON, NEW JERSEY, on the front. The back of the envelope had our address printed on it. I found a stamp and stuck it on. Then I rode my bike to the corner mailbox. Taking a deep breath, I dropped the letter in. Even though I didn't have the exact address, I thought my letter would get to him since he was so famous.

Then I started to worry. How long does it actually take for a letter to get to Princeton, New Jersey?

According to Albert Einstein, time passes at different speeds. Could it take a day, a month, a year? I closed my eyes and wished for the best.

And when my letter gets there, will Albert Einstein even have time to open it?

He'll be solving his own math problems.

Not Annabel's.

Every day for a week, Annabel came home to work on her math problem. She was getting more upset each day.

I never said a word about the letter to Annabel. What if my letter didn't get to him? By now I was angry. Why should big, famous Albert Einstein bother with a little kid like me? What does he care if Annabel fails math?

Just when I was about to give up hope, there it was!  A letter addressed to:
Annabel & her sister
98 Willow Road
Woodmere, New York

I ran to show Annabel.

Annabel opened the envelope. "This is from Albert Einstein!" she burst out. "It's a miracle! Why is he writing to us?" "Simple," I laughed. "I wrote to him and asked him to solve your math problem." She hugged me so hard, I thought I'd explode.

Annabel began to read the letter. "There's no answer here!" She was very disappointed. "I give up." She cried and, throwing the letter down, stormed out of the room. "Wait, Annabel! You can't just quit!" I called. But she had gone.

I picked up the letter and began to read.

"Do not worry about your problems with mathematics, I assure you mine are far greater. Albert Einstein." Is he kidding? I thought. Then I turned the letter over and saw this drawing. Could the drawing be a clue? Maybe it would help Annabel after she calmed down. She didn't come down to dinner, so I went to find her.

She was taking a bath. "Annabel, what if you had a clue to help you find the answer? Would you try to solve your problem?" "I guess," she said. I held up Albert Einstein's drawing. "Look at this," I said. Annabel looked a long time. "Wow," she said. "Maybe I could figure it out." She worked till very late that night. And when I was almost asleep, I heard her say, "I got it!"

The next day, Annabel took the answer to school. The teacher was amazed. "Congratulations, Annabel. How did you do it?" she asked. "Well," confessed Annabel, "I must tell you, I did have a little help from Albert Einstein." "Sure, sure, of course you did," said the teacher with a kindly smile.

But Annabel didn't say a thing. She meant to
keep her secret safe with me and Albert Einstein.

### NOTE

Although he was considered the greatest scientist of the twentieth century, Albert Einstein found time to help local schoolchildren with arithmetic when they came to him. The math problem in this story was actually sent to Albert Einstein by a fifteen-year-old high school girl. He answered her request for help by mail, and the story appeared on the front page of *The New York Times* in May 1952.

The radius of $K_3$ is the difference $r_3 = r_1 - r_2$.

The tangent $O_2 \rightarrow K_3$ is $\parallel$ to the tangent on $K_1$ and $K_2$ and can be easily constructed. This gives the solution.

A. E.

Here is the actual diagram and formula from Albert Einstein. (Mathematicians at the time, while not questioning Einstein's method, said the diagram should have been drawn with the two circles touching.)

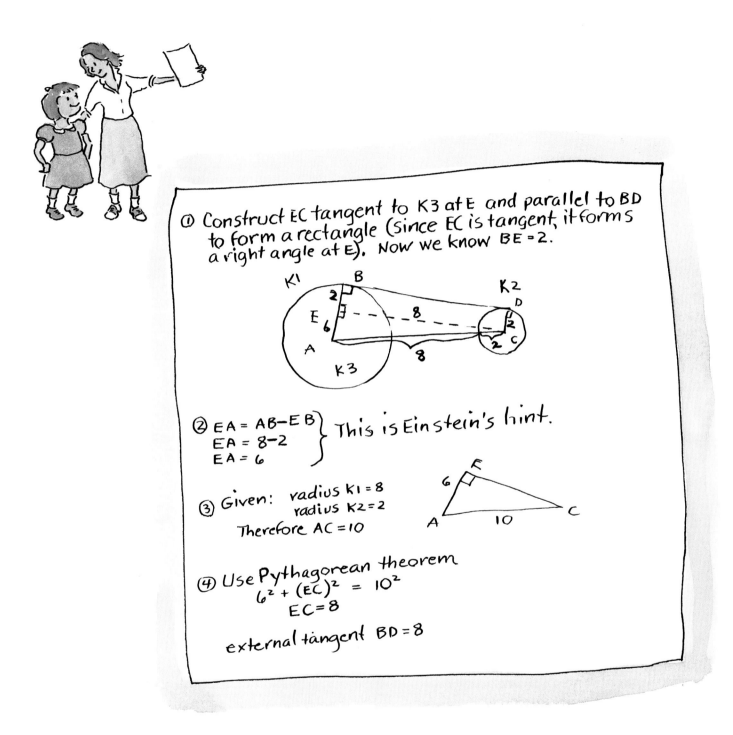

① Construct EC tangent to K3 at E and parallel to BD to form a rectangle (since EC is tangent, it forms a right angle at E). Now we know BE = 2.

K1    B
      2
E   ⌐
  6
A
    K3        8

K2
   D
   2
  2 C

8

② EA = AB−EB ⎫ This is Einstein's hint.
  EA = 8−2  ⎬
  EA = 6    ⎭

③ Given:  radius K1 = 8
          radius K2 = 2
      Therefore AC = 10

      E
   6 ⌐
 A        C
     10

④ Use Pythagorean theorem
    $6^2 + (EC)^2 = 10^2$
        EC = 8

   external tangent BD = 8

This is how Annabel worked out the problem, following Albert Einstein's diagram.

*To Frances Foster and Robbin Gourley, the Dream Team*

Albert Einstein's diagram is reprinted by permission of *The New York Times.*

Distributed in Canada by Douglas & McIntyre Publishing Group
Color separations by Chroma Graphics PTE Ltd.
Printed and bound in the United States of America by Berryville Graphics
Designed by Robbin Gourley
First edition, 2005
1  3  5  7  9  10  8  6  4  2

www.fsgkidsbooks.com

Library of Congress Cataloging-in-Publication Data
Barasch, Lynne.
     Ask Albert Einstein / Lynne Barasch.— 1st ed.
         p.    cm.
     ISBN-13: 978-0-374-30435-5
     ISBN-10: 0-374-30435-1
     1. Einstein, Albert, 1879–1955—Juvenile literature.    I. Title.

QC16.E5B365 2005
530'.092—dc22

                                                           2004047180

"Everything that is really great and inspiring is created by the individual who can labor in freedom."

"I think and think for months and years. Ninety-nine times, the conclusion is false. The hundredth time I am right."